BECAUSE OF Walter

For my dad,
who will have a "whale"
of a time reading this

Contents

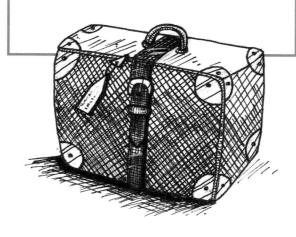

Chapter *1*

I've been in foster care since I was a tiny baby. I don't remember what went on when I was born, but people have told me that my birth mother was very young and couldn't take care of me. They say she put me in foster care while she tried to sort out her life.

I guess she never was able to get it together, though, because I've been in foster homes ever since then. My first foster mother was the absolute best. Her name was Kay, and I really loved her. She seemed so tall and soft, and she had big arms that were always hugging me. She made me feel warm and safe.

Kay is also the person who started calling me Kaysha, even though my name is Michelle on my birth certificate. She said it was what she had always planned on naming her own daughter if she'd ever had one, and that she now wanted to share the name with me.

KAY

I lived with Kay until I was five years old. It was the only home I'd ever known, so I was thrilled when she told me that my real mother had officially put me up for adoption, and that she was going to try to adopt me. But then my world fell apart. It began when Kay started to have to stay in bed all the time. Then doctors started coming and going. Then there were the times that Kay had to go and stay in the hospital.

As these hospital stays grew more frequent, my social worker, Roberta, came to pick me up and take me away. I didn't understand what was going on then, but I later found out that Kay was too sick to adopt me or to even take care of me anymore. Several months later, she died.

By that time, I was in my second home, which lasted for about a year. In fact, from that point on, none of my foster homes seemed to last very long. Ever since I found out that I could be adopted, that's all I ever wanted, but it never seemed to work out. Once, the father of the family I was staying with was transferred to another town. Another time, the couple I was with suddenly had triplets and didn't have room for me anymore.

My last foster home was with the Campbells. They were both veterinarians, and they had an animal clinic in their home. To keep me from getting confused, they had me call them Dr Nan and Dr Greg.

I loved it there. I had a big room all to myself, and they let me help look after the animals that were kept in overnight. I've always loved animals, so it seemed like heaven to me.

I knew this was a home where I wanted to stay. I always tried to be on my best behaviour, and use some of the "survival skills" I'd learned at the other foster homes where I'd stayed. By now, I knew these by heart. Don't touch. Don't steal. Don't talk back. Don't make excuses. Don't make messes. Help out with chores. There were a million of them, and I tried to follow each one. I wanted so badly for it all to work out.

But, as usual, things seemed to go wrong at the worst possible times. Like the time when that huge cat named Muffin came in for an operation. He was the biggest cat I'd ever seen. He looked like a giant striped balloon.

"I hope he won't be too much trouble," his owner said nervously. "Muffin can be a problem."

"Don't worry, we'll cope," Dr Nan said, smiling. "Kaysha here can charm any animal – great or small."

I couldn't believe it. If she thought that, I was in for sure! I proudly walked over to the cage and stuck my fingers in to scratch the cat under the chin. He promptly bit me, but I hardly cared I was so happy.

Muffin's owner reluctantly left, and Dr Nan and I looked at each other.

"We'll have to give him a tranquillizer before we can even start," she said.

I nodded and opened the cage. Muffin bolted out across the examining room like a rocket. Dr Nan and I chased him all over the place until I had a brainstorm. Food! I opened a tin of cat food and put it down. Sure enough, Muffin was a real pushover where food was concerned. From that point on, it was easy, and I felt like Muffin was one of my patients, too.

In fact, that night I went down to check on him. He was sleeping in his cage. I opened it and patted his furry head. He stretched, and purred loudly. I watched him until he went to sleep again, then I crept back upstairs.

The next morning, I heard Dr Nan talking loudly. Then she came bursting into my room.

"Kaysha! You didn't lock the door to Muffin's cage!"

I sat up. "But I'm sure I did..." Then I stopped. She looked really mad, and if there was one thing I'd learned in all of my stays in foster homes, it was never to argue with the adults. That got you bumped out faster than anything, and I wasn't about to do anything to ruin this.

"Well, he's gone, and you've got to help me find him. Now!" Dr Nan said.

Sure enough, the cage door was open, as was the window to the backyard, and Muffin was gone.

In the end, I guess it turned out all right. I finally found Muffin sitting under a tree. He was eating, of course. He'd stolen some of the bread we put out for the birds, and was just munching away happily. I brought him in, locked him up, and breathed a sigh of relief. It looked like everything was OK.

But it wasn't. A couple of days later, Dr Nan and Dr Greg called me into their office and asked me to sit down. They both looked really uncomfortable, and neither one would look me in the eye.

"Um, Kaysha, we're going to adopt…" Dr Greg broke off.

I couldn't hold back. "I know! You want to adopt me! I knew it, I just knew it!" I was ready to start bouncing around the room when I realized that they didn't look very happy about the whole thing. It turned out that they had just been told that they could adopt a little baby girl. They didn't want me after all.

"Kaysha, you're a wonderful girl," Dr Nan choked. I just walked out of the room. I didn't want to hear what I already knew. Nobody wanted to adopt an older kid like me. It was never going to happen. All I could do was pack my things again.

An hour later, my social worker, Roberta, arrived.

"I'm sorry, Kaysha, but you'll have to live at the group home for a while."

I knew what that meant. Social services didn't know where my next foster home was going to be. So I squeezed into a room with six other girls. I longed for privacy, but tried to make the most of things. I did what I always did – I just kept quiet, minded my own business, and hoped for a miracle.

It must have worked. For, after only a week, Roberta told me, "You're going to a new foster home – and this may lead to a permanent placement. The Parkers have one daughter named Victoria, and they can't have any more children. They'd like Victoria to have a sister. If all goes well, Kaysha, you could have a new life!"

Her brown eyes were shining, and I could see that she was really excited. Then she said, "And guess what, Kaysha? Steve Parker is a marine mammal officer, and they live on a beach!"

My heart nearly missed a beat. If anything, this sounded even better than staying with the veterinarians. It was too good to be true. I didn't want to put a jinx on it by showing how excited I was. I'd always wanted to live near the sea.

"The Parkers love animals just like you do, Kaysha," Roberta continued.

I could feel a little tingle of excitement shoot through me. Could this be it?

Chapter 2

I'll never forget the first time I saw the house. The car stopped outside this beautiful, rambling old house. I thought Roberta had forgotten something, or was going to look at her map.

"This is it," she said.

"This is where the Parkers live?" I said, shocked.

"This is where *you* are going to live."

The house was tall and painted white. It had window boxes on the upstairs windows, which were full of bright spring flowers. A vine of pink roses rambled up one of its walls. It had a large front porch, with a friendly, bright blue door right in

the middle. There were tubs of lavender on each side of the stairs.

As we got out of the car, the door opened. They were all there. Mr Parker, Mrs Parker, and Victoria. Mr and Mrs Parker were smiling. Victoria wasn't. She glared at me with small, grey eyes. Mrs Parker asked me to come in and they showed me around the house. It had a cosy entrance hall, full of raincoats and boots, and a huge wooden staircase. There were four bedrooms, and Mr Parker had his own study. My room was blue. It was the prettiest room I'd ever seen. It had an old brass bed with a blue quilt. The wallpaper and curtains were the same blue and white pattern. The best thing about it was the view. From my window I could see the sea.

"Would you like to have a look at the beach, Kaysha?" Mr Parker asked after Roberta had left. "We can walk to it from our house."

I followed him and Victoria down a little path. Before I knew it, there was sand beneath my feet, and the sea was right in front of me.

"Go ahead and take off your shoes," Mr Parker said.

I noticed that Victoria had already removed hers. They looked really expensive. Especially next to my old, hand-me-down sneakers. And then we came to the water's edge. The water stretched far out into the distance until it met the sky, which was almost the same colour. I took in a deep breath of clean sea air. I've always loved the sea. Right then and there, I promised myself that if I got to stay, I'd never take it for granted.

Mr Parker told me about his job as a marine mammal officer. He told me he'd written four books about ocean life, and was now working on one about whales. Victoria said nothing the whole time, so I just listened to him.

"I've had to help sometimes when whales have been stranded," he said.

"Whales get stranded? What do you mean?" I asked.

"They get stuck up on the sand, and when the tide goes out, they often die. No one really knows why it happens, though," Mr Parker said. "One theory is that they get into shallow water and panic. The other whales hear their cries of distress and get stuck, too, when they go to help."

"So the whales talk to each other?" I asked.

"Definitely," he said. "They make all sorts of different sounds. They talk to each other in clicks and groans, and they use sound signals to find their way. Humpback whales can even sing!"

I wanted to ask him more questions, but Victoria spoke for the first time.

"I want to go back, Dad. I'm hungry."

Her voice was whiny. Mr Parker turned back immediately. And I learned something important then. When Victoria wanted something, Victoria got it.

We came back to the house and Shakespeare, the Parkers' big Labrador retriever, jumped all over me. He could tell right from the start that I loved animals. It didn't bother me at all that my first friend in this new house had a long, golden tail.

Things started to go downhill after that. For days, Victoria refused to say anything directly to me. It was only, "Mum, could you tell Kaysha to pass the bread," and other things like that. I could tell she didn't like me. Everywhere I went, I felt her eyes following me. Every time her mum or dad showed me anything, she was always there to change the subject, or ask for something.

I'm coming to the worst part. I'll never forget it. After I'd been there for a week, I took Shakespeare on his daily walk along the beach. When I got back and went into the kitchen, the three Parkers were standing there, arms crossed, glaring at me.

"Why did you do it, Kaysha?" Mr Parker asked.

"Do what?"

"Steal the money!"

My heart started thudding. I didn't know what they were talking about. Mrs Parker put her hands on my shoulders and firmly steered me into my room.

"Does this look familiar?" she asked, as she lifted up the pillow on my bed. There was a twenty-dollar note on the blue sheet. I looked back at them in horror.

"I didn't take that money. I don't steal!" I said, shocked.

Chapter 3

"See – she's a liar, too!" said Victoria in her usual whine. "It's under your pillow, Kaysha. Who else would put it there? The tooth fairy?"

I was too stunned to say anything. Victoria had set me up. I could tell by the way she kept giving me these funny looks, and I could see a little gleam of satisfaction in her eyes. If they believed I was a thief, and a liar as well, there was nothing I could do. I retreated to my usual habit of silence, and I guess the Parkers thought my silence meant I was guilty.

"I'm warning you, Kaysha," said Mrs Parker. "If you ever do this again, I'll have to call Roberta to come and get you. Now we want so much for this to work out, don't we, Victoria?"

"Of course we do," Victoria replied, smiling sweetly.

She was lying through her teeth. You could almost see the lies spitting out through that phony smile. She was really enjoying it, and I knew what she was up to – she wanted me out. It didn't matter what I did or how hard I tried, I was going to get kicked out. Victoria Parker was laying a trap for me.

I decided that as I was going to be leaving, I'd better enjoy the beach as much as I could in whatever time I had left. I went for a long walk after dinner. It had been a really nice meal – lamb chops and new potatoes – but I had a hard time getting through it. As I climbed up the path, I took off my shoes. My feet made little patterns in the sand. Then

I waded through the water. The waves roared in my ears, and far in the distance I could see a tiny speck that was an island.

As I put on my shoes, my new teacher walked past with her dachshund. I smiled to myself because they really looked like they belonged together. They were both short, and had little legs.

"Hello, Kaysha," she said.

"Hello, Mrs Peters," I said. I already liked her. She had done a lot to make me feel welcome that first week.

"See that island out there?" she said. "It's called Whale Point."

"Whale Point?" I was immediately interested.

"Whales often swim past it. One time, nearly two hundred pilot whales were counted!"

"Really?" I tried to imagine that many whales. "I wish I could see a whale. I've never seen one before," I said sadly. Then, to my surprise, I found myself telling her what I had seen, and people I had known. "So this is just about my last chance," I concluded. "If the Parkers don't want me, chances are no one will. People just want to adopt babies, not nine-year-old foster kids like me."

"Well, dear, the Parkers are wonderful people. Just be patient, and I think something good will happen," she said, and patted my shoulder. "Roly! Come here!" That was her dog's name. Roly Poly. He raced up and started jumping all over me with his sandy paws.

"I don't mind," I said, laughing. And I didn't. I patted him while he wagged his long pencil of a tail.

"I think he likes you," said Mrs Peters.

"He knows that I like him." Then I realized why I always liked animals so much. They liked me no matter what happened. They liked me just for being me.

When I got back to the house, Victoria was watching a video, Mr Parker was researching in his study, and Mrs Parker was training more roses up the trellis. I offered to help, but she said she didn't mind doing them herself. So I walked upstairs to my room, lay on my bed, and stared at the ceiling. I knew I was sitting on a time bomb. It wouldn't be long before the next thing happened, and I'd be blamed.

I didn't have to wait long. Two days later there was a cry from upstairs. We all ran to where Mrs Parker was standing by her open jewellery box.

"My necklace is gone!" she cried.

I could feel my heart start thudding. Here it comes.

"Kaysha, did you do this?" she asked.

As I shook my head, Mr Parker rubbed his forehead.

"I'll go and check her room," Victoria chirped.

I knew Victoria would find it. She knew exactly where it was. She came back triumphant.

"I can't find the necklace, but I found one of your matching earrings on the floor, Mum. She took the necklace and hid it. She's not stupid enough to put it in her room again!"

"Kaysha, please tell me where it is!" said Mrs Parker. "I promise if you return it, we'll do nothing further about it."

I felt sick – I was trapped. I couldn't give the necklace back because I didn't know where Victoria had hidden it.

Chapter 4

I got the cold shoulder for the rest of the day. I kept thinking that maybe, just maybe, I could beat Victoria at her own game. If I could just find where she had hidden the necklace. But where would she put it? Certainly not in my room. What about her room?

So I watched and waited. When Victoria went to play a computer game with her father, I carefully opened her bedroom door. I felt really guilty doing it, as one of my survival rules had always been to leave other people's stuff alone. But I was desperate.

Her room was a pink version of mine. The bed was the same kind and the walls

and curtains had a similar pattern. She had a collection of porcelain dolls on the window-sill. They were beautiful. Hands clasped behind my back, I tiptoed over to them and looked. There were about fifteen of them, and one looked exactly like Victoria.

"What are you doing?" snapped Mrs Parker from behind me. I slowly turned, my stomach sinking into my shoes.

"Come with me," she continued.

I followed her to Mr Parker's study. He was still playing the game with Victoria.

"Kaysha was in your room, Victoria."

"I was just looking at the dolls," I said.

Mr Parker relaxed. "They are pretty, aren't they?" he said.

I nodded. There was a pause. I could hear the clock ticking. Then Mr Parker said very quietly, "Kaysha, please give back the necklace."

I smiled weakly and fought back the tears that were welling up in my eyes. I was beaten. I'd never find it. Like a dog with its tail between its legs, I walked out.

The next day I took Shakespeare for a walk along the beach. He loved it. He ran along the wet sand, barking at the seagulls. None of them paid much attention, except for one fat one that pecked his leg. That made Shakespeare go berserk. He yapped and yelped and ran around in circles.

I was about to take him home when I saw them. At first I couldn't believe my eyes. I kept thinking I was imagining it. But there they were – a group of whales by Whale Point. I could see them away in the distance. Everybody on the beach was excitedly pointing and walking into the water to get a better look. One man was taking pictures. He took so many I saw him reload his camera. And then they were gone. The black, shadowy shapes had disappeared into the horizon.

"Wow! That's a lot of whales!" said a little fair-haired boy.

People stood for a while, gazing out to sea then, one by one, they walked away.

I turned to go, too, when I noticed that Shakespeare was missing.

"Shakespeare!" I yelled. I whistled loudly. Another dog looked up at me, but Shakespeare was gone. Great. The Parkers were already upset – I'd be out for sure if I lost their dog.

"Shakespeare!" I called, running up towards our path. Maybe he'd gone home,

I thought frantically. He wasn't interested in whales. Then I saw him. He was digging by a tree on our path. I rushed over to him.

"Shakespeare! Don't ever do that to me again!" I said, as I tried to haul him home. He started to pull and bark, and then I saw what he'd been digging for – the missing necklace!

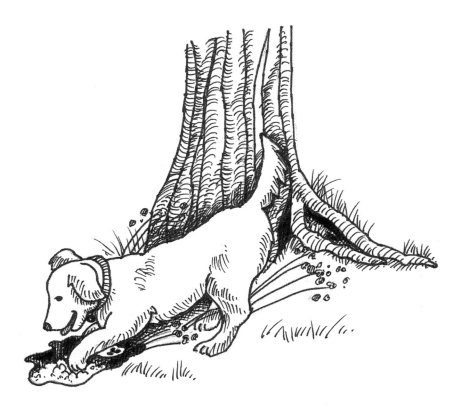

Chapter 5

There it was, sparkling in the dirt. I brushed it off, thinking it was almost too good to be true. Victoria had hidden it, but my friend Shakespeare had found it. I put it in my pocket and followed Shakespeare home.

It was a Sunday, and Mrs Parker had cooked a roast. I'd broken another one of my survival rules – never be late – and I knew they'd all be sitting at the table, waiting for me. I opened the old, glass-panelled dining room doors.

Sure enough, they were all there. Three heads turned towards me. Three pairs of eyes coldly met mine. I was bursting with excitement, but I kept pushing it down. I took my hand from my pocket and quietly placed the necklace on the table. There was a pause. They looked at the necklace shining on the tablecloth. Mrs Parker smiled, Mr Parker nodded his head, and Victoria just sat there with her mouth wide open. She was too

shocked to say anything. Mrs Parker picked up the necklace, patted my shoulder, and went upstairs to put it away.

"Thank you, Kaysha," said Mr Parker. "We knew we could count on you for this."

It had been years since anyone had been so kind to me.

Mrs Parker came back and dished out the meal. Victoria hardly touched hers, but I practically inhaled it. After I'd enthusiastically eaten five extra roast potatoes, I remembered the whales.

"I'm really sorry I was late for dinner, but there was a large group of whales by Whale Point!"

Mr Parker looked up, immediately interested. "How many?"

"I didn't count, but I heard a lady say there must have been at least forty."

"That's probably the same pod of pilot whales that have been sighted further down the coast."

"Why do they call a group of whales a pod? That's pretty stupid – only peas come in a pod," mumbled Victoria. She was in an awful mood. She curled her lip and I could see her pink gums above her teeth.

"Well, if you prefer, you could call it a school or a herd, Victoria," Mr Parker said calmly. Then he ignored her and turned back to me. "Shall we go and have a look?"

I was excited. Victoria was furious. She got up and slammed the glass-panelled doors. I held my breath, expecting them to shatter. They didn't. Mr Parker acted as though nothing had happened. He helped Mrs Parker carry the dishes into the kitchen.

"Why don't you come for a walk with Kaysha and me?"

"OK," she said, and smiled warmly at me.

Shakespeare excitedly followed us along the path. The beach was almost deserted. It was chilly and the wind tossed the waves angrily over the sand.

"They were over there." I pointed to the island.

Mr Parker pulled out his binoculars. He spent a while looking intently through them while Shakespeare chased a seagull.

"They're gone, all right," said Mr Parker. "They might not be back. It's spring, so the pilot whales are following their leaders from warm to cold waters."

"There were a lot of them," I said.

"Forty isn't that big a group. Pilots can travel in pods of almost a thousand."

The three of us spent about an hour sitting on the beach. Shakespeare eventually gave up on the seagull. I think he finally got the point – seagulls could fly, but he couldn't.

I got the biggest surprise of my life later that evening. Victoria came into my room with a big smile on her face.

"Mum and Dad say you and I should try and be friends," she said.

She took me up to her room and showed me all her dolls, and then she let me look at her collection of shells. She had been collecting them ever since she was a young child. And she had something to say about every one of them. Then we watched a movie on TV. For the first time in months, I went to bed that night feeling really good. I fell asleep listening to the waves rhythmically wash over the beach.

A couple of days later, after we got home from school, Victoria asked me to look at her school project.

"Now tell me what you really think," she said, as we went up the stairs, snacks in hand.

"I'm not an expert," I said hesitantly. I was still surprised whenever she was friendly, and I didn't want to blow it.

"Well, Mrs Peters will have to like it, because it's about dachshunds," Victoria said with her mouth full.

I followed her into her room and she pulled out her project from her desk drawer. She spread it out over the bed. It was wonderful. Victoria could really draw. She'd done a series of cartoons featuring a dachshund, and she'd painted a beautiful picture of Roly Poly.

"It's amazing!" I said.

"Do you know what I'm going to do with it?" she said, smiling.

"No."

Her face changed. "I'm going to rip it up!"

"Victoria, no!" I said. I couldn't believe this was happening.

She snarled, "I'm going to rip it and say it's your fault! I just pretended to be your friend. I don't want you here! I want my parents to myself!"

She started tearing up the project. I reached over to try to stop her.

"Victoria, don't!"

It was too late. Victoria had ripped it and now she was tearing it to shreds in a mad frenzy.

"Victoria, stop it!" I shouted.

Then Victoria started yelling. "No! Stop it, Kaysha! Mum!"

The door opened. Mrs Parker stood looking at us.

"What's wrong?"

"Kaysha ripped up my project! She did it because it was better than hers. I told you she hates me, Mum! I wish she'd go away!" She threw herself onto the bed and cried loudly. I stared down at the trail of ripped paper.

"Tell me, Kaysha, did you do this?" Mrs Parker asked me, with a look of sharp disappointment.

"No, I didn't. She did."

Victoria looked up and gave an enormous sob. "She's just saying that, Mum, because she was so jealous of my picture. I spent weeks doing it. I was going to surprise Mrs Peters."

"Kaysha, I think you'd better go to your room. I'm afraid I will have to call Roberta. We let you off the hook about the stealing, but this is inexcusable. You're not even trying to fit in."

I turned and walked towards the door. Then I looked back. Mrs Parker was picking up the pieces and shaking her head. Victoria looked at me with a smug smile. I knew it was useless trying to say anything. It would just sound like more excuses. Victoria had won.

Shakespeare must have known that something was wrong. He came into my room, put his head on my shoulder, and made little wheezing and whining noises. He stayed in my room with me, even when I didn't go down for dinner. I patted his golden, silky ears over and over again. I didn't know what else to do. I was going to be kicked out again, and I might never have another chance to get adopted.

It must have been hours later when I heard a loud banging on the front door. I sat up. Shakespeare had gone and I could hear him barking downstairs. Then there was silence. Curiosity got the better of me. It was really late, and I wondered who could be at the door. I tiptoed down the stairs and saw Mr and Mrs Parker talking to a man in a wet brown jacket.

"Steve, there must be nearly fifty of them, all stranded on the beach."

"I'll call some people I know who can help," Mr Parker responded.

"What's wrong?" asked Victoria, who rushed down the stairs past me.

"Beached pilot whales!" said the man.

"Can I help?" I asked.

"We'll all go. We'll be needed down there!" Mrs Parker said. She gave me one of the jackets from the entrance hall and a torch, and I followed her and Victoria down to the beach.

I couldn't believe my eyes. The entire beach was covered in black whales, all desperately fighting for their lives.

Chapter 6

It was dark, but a full moon cast eerie shadows over the whales. Their magnificent, shining black bodies – some of them as large as a school bus – were sprawled helplessly over the sand. There were about a dozen people hovering over them with lanterns and torches.

I knelt beside one. His eyes were shut tightly. They blended with the bumps on his head. Every few minutes, he exhaled his warm breath through the blowhole at the top of his head. I wanted to help him. I'd never touched a whale before, but without hesitating, I just bent over and pressed my face against his warm, wet body. For an instant, he seemed to respond. I could sense that something passed between us. He knew I was going to help him. I stroked him gently and, at that moment, he was my friend. I decided to call him Walter.

"Don't worry, Walter, we're going to get you back home. I know what it's like to be in a strange place and afraid."

I heard voices and saw dozens of people coming down our path. Mr Parker was in front in a wet suit and he was talking intently with the group of serious-faced people who were following him.

"I'd like your attention, please," he called to the rest of the people on the beach.

Everyone looked at him silently.

"I'm a marine mammal officer, and I have asked these experts from the Department of Conservation to help us. It's very important that we follow correct procedures. If we mess up, the whales could die."

I heard a whispering cough among the people, and I hugged Walter again.

"Now, we need to keep the whales calm," continued Mr Parker. "We need to prevent any loud noises from scaring them. And, most importantly, we need to keep them wet by pouring sea water over them. I've arranged for a truckload of towels that we can soak and use to cover them. Keep their blowholes and eyes clear at all times. We have to wait until the next high tide before we can refloat them. There are a few still out at sea. It's important that they don't beach, too."

I looked out to sea and I thought I could see the black shapes in the distance.

Mr Parker came over to me. "It looks like this whale likes you," he said, kneeling beside me. Then Victoria joined him.

"He's beautiful!" said Victoria. She stroked the whale with gentle fingers.

"It's important to keep him wet and cool until high tide," said Mr Parker.

"How long is that, Dad?" asked Victoria.

"Ten o'clock tomorrow morning."

"Dad, that's eleven hours away!"

"That's why it's really important to keep this whale wet. Do you think you two can handle it?"

"Yes!" Victoria and I said at exactly the same time.

"His name is Walter," I told her quietly.

"Hello, Walter," she whispered.

Mr Parker left us with Walter and he moved around among the other whales and organized the volunteers. A truck drove onto the beach and towels were given to everybody. I didn't want to leave Walter. I was worried that if I left him for one second he would feel alone and afraid.

"I'll soak the towels in sea water," said Victoria. She went to the water and came back a few moments later and together we draped the wet towels over Walter's long body. He stirred. It was almost as if he was telling us that he liked the feel of the wet towels. Then some buckets arrived and Victoria and I filled and refilled them tirelessly, pouring the water over him. Every time the water touched him, Walter moved his sleek black flipper. It was like a nod of approval.

"Hang in there, Walter. You're going to make it," I said.

"You bet!" added Victoria.

Both of us put our heads against him.

Suddenly, it hit me. Victoria wasn't acting like an enemy anymore. She was helping me help Walter. We were all in it together, Victoria, Walter, and I, and it felt like we were becoming friends at last.

We worked together for hours, without saying much. Dawn came. The sun slowly rose over the horizon. After our long, cold night, it was like a display of golden fireworks. Then a van arrived on the beach with huge pots of hot soup and loaves of warm, crusty bread, all provided by the local bakery.

"I don't want to leave Walter," I said.

"Don't worry – I'll get the food for us," said Victoria.

She came back minutes later with a tray full of food. We were so hungry, we gobbled up bowl after bowl of soup.

"Not long till high tide," Victoria said.

I looked at my watch. It was nearly seven o'clock.

Chapter 7

As it got lighter, everything seemed more hopeful. But, suddenly, I noticed that Walter wasn't moving his flipper very much. And his breathing was becoming slower and slower.

"Something's wrong," I said.

Victoria grew pale. "Wait – let me go and get Dad!"

I put my arm around Walter. "Come on, boy!" I pleaded. I looked at him. He was very still. "There's only three more hours to go. You have to make it, Walter!"

Mr Parker came over to us. "What's wrong?" He knelt down and touched Walter. "He's starting to dry out. I'll call the vet."

He disappeared for a few minutes, and then he came back with the vet.

"Girls, this is Dr Gosney. He's going to have a look."

Dr Gosney ran his hands over Walter. He paused while they rested on Walter's underside, then he shook his head.

"I'm sorry, but I don't think this whale's going to make it."

"Why not?" Victoria and I both said at the same time.

"He's quite an old male whale. He was perhaps one of the first to become disoriented and beach himself. He's been out of the water too long. There are three others that are in the same condition."

"Is there any hope for him at all?" I asked quietly.

"I don't think so."

I could see Dr Gosney was upset. "He's a magnificent old boy!" he said.

"He's Walter!" said Victoria, and the tears rolled down her face.

I put my head against Walter. I had started to cry, too, and my tears made little wet patterns on his warm black skin.

"Just try and keep him as wet as possible," said Dr Gosney.

Victoria and I went into overdrive. We raced up and down the beach with buckets of water and slopped them over Walter. We must have poured at least a hundred of them when we both flopped down on the sand. Then Walter feebly waved his flipper. It was weak, but it was progress! Both of us put our arms around him.

"You're not giving up, are you, Walter?" I whispered.

Then Victoria jumped up. She called out, "This whale might make it if we can get him really wet!"

Suddenly, there was water coming from everywhere. One man used his hands to dig a trench around Walter, and I poured water into it.

The tide was coming in faster now. It crept up the beach, lapping against the sand. It moved a little further up the beach each time the waves rolled ashore.

"We can start refloating them!" Mr Parker finally yelled.

Tirelessly, everyone began pushing the whales as the tide washed in around them. We had to turn Walter towards the sea.

"They're going to need at least half an hour of gentle rocking in the water to get back their balance and ease their muscles," Mr Parker told everyone.

"How's Walter doing?" I heard Dr Gosney ask.

"He's not responding much," I said worriedly.

"He's not doing anything!" said Victoria.

"Is he dead?" I asked.

Dr Gosney looked at him. "No, he's very much alive! He's surprised me!"

"Does he have a chance?" I asked.

"Yes!"

With a group of helpers, we rocked Walter back and forth in the water. His body felt rubbery and smooth against our fingers.

"How do we get them to swim out?" I asked.

"That's the problem," said Dr Gosney. "Sometimes they don't."

"What happens then?" I asked with a feeling of dread.

Dr Gosney's face was grim. "Well, they often don't survive a second beaching. That's the real tragedy."

No one said anything after that. We just kept rocking Walter.

"You're going to make it!" I said.

That's when it happened. Suddenly, a school of dolphins headed for shore, and all the whales began to respond. I could see they were starting to communicate with each other. The dolphins were guiding the whales to safety, just like the lights on a runway guide planes. They steered the whales to sea.

One by one, the whales swam off into the sea. Walter made a supreme effort. He lifted his head high as we gave him a push.

Then he was off. Our Walter disappeared into the sea with his friends.

"He made it!" I cried.

"And we helped him!" said Victoria.

She and I hugged each other. Mr and Mrs Parker hugged both of us, too.

"You helped save him – he couldn't have done it without you!"

Chapter 8

You should have heard the people on the beach. Anybody would think they were at a party instead of on a beach after a sleepless night of nursing whales. Everybody was hugging each other. I saw photographers and television cameras everywhere. I noticed a helicopter noisily hovering above us.

We all walked home and I went to bed. I slept until six o'clock that evening. When I woke up, I noticed that it was quiet upstairs. Down below, I heard a car pull up. I went into the hall and looked out the window. It was Roberta. Then I remembered – I had to leave. I returned to my room, put the few things I owned into my bag, and went quietly down the stairs. In the front room, I saw Roberta sitting with the Parkers.

"Kaysha, come in here, please," said Roberta.

I sat down without looking at anyone. This time leaving really hurt, especially after we had all worked together so well last night.

"Kaysha, the Parkers have made a decision." I knew what was coming next, and I didn't want to hear it. "They want to legally adopt you."

I must have heard it wrong. "What?"

"We want you to live with us permanently," said Mr Parker.

I looked up.

"I want you to be my sister," said Victoria. "I'm really sorry about all those awful things I did. I couldn't sleep until I told Mum and Dad everything. I was just so jealous because I'd always had Mum and Dad to myself. Can you forgive me?"

And so I stayed. I've been here a year now. Victoria's the best friend I ever could have hoped for. We spend hours on the beach, talking and watching for whales. We've never given up hope that Walter will swim past one day. We think about him often. Victoria has drawn some beautiful pictures of him. One was chosen to be on the cover of our local phone book.

Because of Walter, all of our lives have changed. Yes, maybe we helped him when he needed it, but he helped me even more. He gave me my family.

From the Author

One day, I saw an article in the newspaper about some whales that were stranded on a New Zealand beach. The local people kept the whales wet, but couldn't get them to swim out to sea. Finally, some dolphins came to the rescue and guided the whales to open water.

I thought a good story could be made out of this article, so I spent time in the library reading and learning about whales and why they get stranded. I love whales and I would really love to be able to help in such a rescue effort. Perhaps, one day, I'll get that chance!

Carol Krueger

From the Illustrator

I was born in Enschede, Holland, but grew up in
north-eastern Oklahoma. For several years, I also lived in
Heidelberg, Germany. I've always felt that my European
background has strongly influenced my work.

I received my Bachelor of Fine Arts in Commercial Art
from the University of Kansas. Since then, my career
has included illustrating greeting cards, working as a
computer graphic designer, and teaching illustration
and design. Recently, I turned my hand to illustrating
children's books. I live in Colorado Springs, Colorado.

Mary Dahl Winton

Because of Walter

ISBN 13: 978-157257673-5
ISBN 10: 157257673-1

 Kingscourt

Published by:
McGraw-Hill Education
Shoppenhangers Road, Maidenhead, Berkshire, England, SL6 2QL
Telephone: 44 (0) 1628 502730
Fax: 44 (0) 1628 635895
Website: www.kingscourt.co.uk
Website: www.mcgraw-hill.co.uk

Written by **Carol Krueger**
Illustrated by **Mary Dahl Winton**
Edited by **Rebecca McEwen**
Designed by **Pat Madorin**

Original Edition © 1997 Shortland Publications
English Reprint Edition © 2009 McGraw Hill Publishing Company

Printed in China through Colorcraft Ltd., Hong Kong

The **McGraw·Hill** Companies